Talk to Strangers

Börkur Sigurbjörnsson

Talk to Strangers

Urban Volcano

Talk to Strangers
Börkur Sigurbjörnsson

Cover: Ana Piñeyro
Illustrations: Börkur Sigurbjörnsson
Publisher: Urban Volcano

https://urbanvolcano.net/

ISBN 978-9935-9466-3-8

Contents

The Businessman Who Gave His Guitar Away

"Señor Manuel Sánchez, please contact a member of the staff at gate number fifteen," a slightly irritated voice sounded through the loudspeaker system.

My eyes wandered toward the desk at gate number fifteen. A middle-aged woman sat in her chair, surveying the waiting area like a prison guard in her watchtower, waiting to detect any unexpected movement in response to her call. Nobody stood up. No one came forward.

It was the tenth time or so that this same person had been asked to contact airline personnel. What was going on? I had spent quite some time waiting at airports in my life, but I had never been requested to speak to the staff at the gate. Not through the loudspeaker system, at least. I did not quite get why people needed to be called to the gate before boarding began. Was there anything more to be said about the reservation? Was the transaction not already complete? The passengers were most likely already checked in. Was there any reason to check them out further?

Neither did I understand why people recurrently did not show up in time—why their name had to be repeated over and over again. Was there a connection between the two? Did the people called to the desk have a reason not to show up? Or did I merely pay attention to the ones who did not answer the call since their names were repeated continuously? I had no clue. The behavioral patterns of missing airline passengers were not among my specialist subjects.

I reached for my leather Burberry briefcase and took out my Moleskine notebook and my favorite Montblanc pen. I decided to make good use of my time and prepare a list of things I needed to do upon returning to the faculty. I should write a short report for my colleagues, describing my experience at the conference. Also, I needed to take a good look at the paper by the group from Cornell. Their talk had been very interesting, the research appeared to be remarkably solid, and the presentation style was highly entertaining. It seemed so easy for those Ivy League scholars to produce one masterpiece after another. They had access to resources far beyond what I could ever dream of in Madrid. If only there were a way for me to collaborate with such a highly regarded institute. I could imagine myself attending a first-class conference as a speaker rather than merely playing the role of spectator as I had done in Santiago.

I looked up from my notebook and over the waiting area, imagining I was scanning a crowded conference hall, filled with an audience excited to hear me present my groundbreaking research. I visualized myself onstage, dressed in a gray suit, a light-blue shirt, and a crimson tie. I was wearing black shoes and the stage lights reflected off the well-polished leather. I held my head up high and cleared my throat. "Good morning, ladies and gentlemen," I began. "It is a great pleasure for me to be here today to present my joint research with my colleagues from Cornell University."

"Señor Manuel Sánchez, please contact a member of the staff at gate number fifteen."

The announcement brought me out of my daydream, knocked me off the podium and threw me back into my seat at gate number fifteen of El Dorado International Airport. Once again they were calling out for the mysterious passenger, Señor Manuel Sánchez. If bets were to be taken, I would say he was sleeping at some other gate after having had too much to drink. How could people otherwise go missing at airports? It was not as if we were in the middle of a great wilderness. At least not here in Bogotá. Maybe people got lost at the big airports with their numerous multistory terminals and long corridors that wound round like snakes in a desert, like Heathrow or Barajas, but not at El Dorado.

"I wonder what happened to Señor Sánchez!"

I looked at the man who had addressed me. He sat to my left and leaned forward over the two empty seats between us. A short fellow with a small round face, tan skin, and thin black hair that was combed back but failed to properly cover a bald patch at the rear of his head. A sparse but neatly trimmed mustache decorated his upper lip. He was wearing a ragged dark-blue tracksuit a size or two too big for his slender body. The hoodie was unzipped, revealing a crumpled T-shirt that might have been considered white a few hundred washes ago. The same could have been said about his shabby running shoes of somewhat indeterminate color. His smile gave him a boyish look, barring a line of crooked, coffee-stained teeth.

“You know Señor Sánchez?” I asked.

“Everybody knows Señor Sánchez,” said the man, grinning. “Sánchez is a very common name.”

“But do you know this particular Señor Sánchez? Señor Manuel Sánchez?“

“I doubt that I do. As I said, Sánchez is a very common name.”

I nodded and waited for a few moments to see if the man intended to continue the dialogue that had, until now, been rather meagre. As he showed no sign of proceeding, I returned to writing my to-do list.

I noted that I should ask Alba to return my copy of John Locke’s *Second Treatise*. I found it strange that she had not already given it back to me. She was a bright student, and given that the book had a chapter on property, it was especially ironic that she had not respected my ownership of the book and had kept it for several weeks.

“Going to Mexico City?” the man asked when I had barely touched my pen upon the notebook paper.

“No,” I replied, faking a friendly smile in order to hide my irritation at being disturbed once again. “I’m on my way to Madrid. My flight is the next one leaving from this gate. The one after Mexico City, that is.”

“White blood in my veins, pure football in my heart, *¡Hala Madrid!*” the man chanted. “Did you like Colombia?”

"I haven't really been to Colombia," I confessed. "My business here in Bogotá is merely a stopover. This morning I flew in from Santiago. Santiago de Chile."

"Ah, Chile. Serious people, the Chileans. They do serious business. You know? You can grasp a lot about how people do business by looking." The man nodded his head and pointed at his eyes. "I've been looking at how people do business here in Colombia. Observing people's behavior. Looking at how they go about their dealings. The Colombian style of trading is completely different from how we do things back home in Mexico. Are you a businessman yourself? Were you doing business in Chile?"

"Yes and no," I replied. "I'm a professor. My main research area is in the field of business administration, but I don't practice business, as such. My interests are mainly of a scholarly nature. I was attending an academic conference in Santiago."

"Ah, a scholar," said the man, raising his eyebrows and nodding his head. "I was never much of an academic. It was hard for the teachers to shove knowledge into my head. It was full of its own ideas, that mind. There wasn't much room for the teachers' wisdom. Always been more interested in action than books. My son, however, was a computer science student in Mexico City. A good one. Clever kid. Top grades. Maybe a bit too clever for his teachers' liking.

Created a gambling site and ran it on the campus network. The professors didn't appreciate that sort of entrepreneurial ambition. They expelled him. Can you imagine?"

"I'm sorry to hear that," I lied, thinking that I would certainly have sided with my Mexican colleagues. An academic institute was no place to run a dodgy business like a gambling site.

"Life is too short to be sorry. It was just as well they expelled him. He was too clever to waste his time attending classes. The affair gave us a chance to start doing business together. Father and son."

"What sort of business?" I asked, trying to imagine the genre of enterprise a man in this outfit could possibly be involved in. "Maybe an off-campus gambling site?"

"No," the man replied, laughing. "We're building a finance website. With financial advice, investments, and insurance. A simple site. Rich in content but succinct and up to date. There's a gap in the market for that sort of thing in Mexico."

I nodded and gave him an encouraging smile even though his description had failed to impress me. For a moment I thought about explaining to him that maneuvering in the financial market was anything but a simple affair. All research indicated that it was not possible to explain the topic on a simple website.

However, I was eager to get back to planning for my return to the Old World and decided to leave the discussion at that, hoping he would do the same.

"Colombia is a really nice place," the man said, wiping out my hope of terminating the dialogue. He reached into his pocket for a bulky point-and-shoot camera and moved one seat closer.

"This is the main square in Chiquinquirá," he continued, turning the camera display toward me, flipping through the photos. "And this is a cat I saw on a side street."

I could not see much of the photos as the camera was not quite the latest model and the display was small. I could only guess I was not missing all that much.

"This is yours truly in his fancy suit," he added, handing me the camera so I could confirm for myself the incredible wardrobe statement, "before it got stolen."

The photo was taken in a square and the man posed in front of a fountain. He was wearing a blue suit over a truly white shirt. Like his tracksuit, the attire was worn and way too big for his skinny body. In one hand he held a black fake leather sports bag with a gold-colored Adidas logo. From behind his back the neck of a guitar stuck out.

"How did your clothes get stolen?" I asked as I gave the camera back. Having seen the man wearing garments that went in the direction of being possibly considered somewhat decent, I could almost relate to him. Maybe he was a businessman after all, albeit not of the caliber I was used to mingling with.

"I was taking a shower at my hostel one morning when they stole my suit," the businessman explained, putting the camera back into his pocket. "Fortunately, I always take my passport, wallet, and other valuable essentials with me to the shower."

"It must have been quite an inconvenience, having your suit stolen," I sympathized, feeling truly sorry for the man having to resort to this hideous tracksuit.

"Nah. They were not that fancy. Not that I need fancy clothes. Or much clothing, for that matter. I like to travel light. I started my trip with a bag and my guitar. This is all my luggage at the end of the trip." The businessman lifted a crumpled white plastic bag that looked practically empty.

"They stole the guitar too?"

"No," the businessman said, smiling. "The fate of the guitar... that's quite another story."

As hopeful as I had been a few minutes ago that the man would shut up, I had to admit that now I was rather curious to know what had happened to the guitar and hoped the businessman would continue his story. And so he did.

"I was walking along the main street in a village near Chiquinquirá when a tramp came up to me. 'Señor, you want the best food in town? Señor, come with me to have the best food in town.' I followed him across the street to a small family run restaurant, sat down, and ordered a *bandeja paisa*. Can you imagine? Myself with a massive *bandeja paisa?* Anyway... the vagrant sat down at the next table and the waiter brought him a beer. I guessed that was the deal. He brought in customers and got paid with a drink. I imagine that's what you scholars call remunerative incentive, or something like that."

"We might," I confirmed, rather surprised by his knowledge of economic terminology, although I would not have used as lavish a phrase for such a cheap exchange.

"As I was waiting for my food to arrive, I grabbed my guitar and played a *ranchera* my father taught me when I was a kid. When the food arrived I put my guitar aside and the tramp looked up from his beer and clapped. 'You sing very well, Señor.' I thanked him and offered him my guitar while I ate. The vagrant reached out for the guitar, closed his eyes, and started playing. He sang about his life. He sang about his sorrows. His voice was soft and his tune had good harmony. I ate my meal with pleasure. The tramp was right, it was undoubtedly the best feast in town. To top it all off, it was accompanied by excellent musical entertainment.

"The waiter brought me coffee, and the tramp attempted to return the guitar. 'Keep it,' I insisted despite his resistance and arguing it was mine and he was going to give it back. 'Play on,' I encouraged him, 'play for me while I drink my coffee.' The tramp closed his eyes again and continued to play the sad and beautiful songs. Meanwhile, I took a big sip of my coffee, put money on the table, and stood up as quietly as I could. Tiptoeing out of the restaurant, I left the guitar in the hands of the tramp."

"You gave your guitar away?" I asked, slightly surprised to hear how careless he was of his possessions. First the suit and now the guitar.

"Sure I did. The tramp deserved the guitar much more than I do. He had so many more sorrows to sing about."

"Flight AV44 to Mexico City is now ready for boarding," airline staff announced, and people started queuing to get on board.

"Well, that's it then," the man said and prepared to leave. "My business here in Colombia is over. It's time for me to head back home."

We saluted each other and the businessman walked slowly in his oversize tracksuit, crumpled plastic bag in hand, toward gate number fifteen and mixed in with

the crowd that had lined up for their flight to Mexico
City.

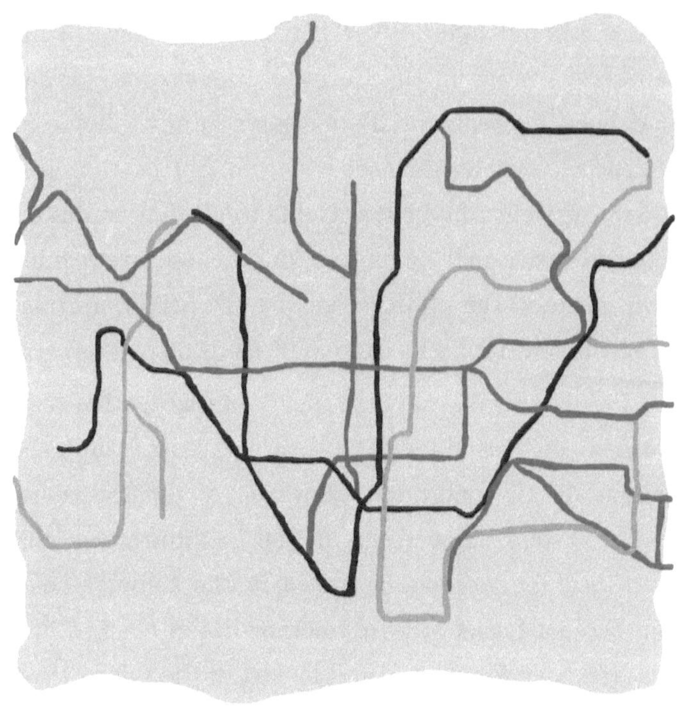

Philip walked onto the central platform of the Glòries station. It was early in the evening and the platform was not very crowded, making it easy for him to navigate to the farthest side. He had a preference for that end. He did not know why. It was not intentional or based on some elaborate reasoning, he just always found his way to that side without thinking about a motive. Maybe it was related to the fact that all his life Philip had had to contemplate his place among the people around him. What had been his place in his motherless home in the Cornwall countryside? What had been his place at his mother's family's home in Valencia?—where his mother had in fact been mostly absent as well. Maybe it was due to all that confusion and insecurity that he unconsciously chose to stake his own place on the platform among the people waiting. It was in his nature to carve out his own space.

Philip wiped away the pearl of sweat that had formed on his forehead since walking onto the minimally air-conditioned platform of the Barcelona metro system. The trains in the Mediterranean city were usually thoroughly cooled in the summer heat, but the platforms were an inferno. Philip reached into his backpack for a book and looked at the information screen. The next train would arrive in forty seconds, so he did not bother to open the book. The wait would be too short to get engaged with a character or a plot before being interrupted by the act of stepping onto the train.

"Did you know that female penguins leave their eggs with the male while they search for food for themselves?" asked a tall dark-haired woman standing next to Philip. She had a look of corporate success, wearing a neat suit and carrying a stylish briefcase.

"How do you know?" replied a short blond-haired woman with pierced eyebrows, wearing jeans and a T-shirt, carrying a worn backpack. A snake tattoo peeked out from under her shirt and seemed to be climbing up the back of her neck.

"Saw it in a documentary," claimed the tall woman, glancing at her expensive-looking wristwatch.

"But that makes no sense. Wouldn't it be better to send the bloke to look for food? Antarctic takeaway, or something?"

"Nah. That's old fashioned. This is a kind of declaration of independence. Girl power."

The two women could hardly look more different from each other and Philip wondered what their relationship was. Judging by the location and time of day, he would have guessed they were colleagues, but based on their highly diverging outfits, it was more likely they were friends—or lovers.

Philip was not able to follow the rest of the women's discussion through the noise of the train that rattled from the tunnel into the station, sending a squeaky sound through the air as the brakes gripped the wheels.

★ ★ ★ ★ ★

Philip leaned against the door of the train and opened his book. His travel companion these days was a collection of short stories by W. Somerset Maugham—a book he had stumbled upon in a secondhand English bookstore a few days earlier. As the train started moving, he dove into the story he had been reading on his commute to work.

... Mrs Hamlyn passed Pryce on the deck ...

Who was Mrs. Hamlyn again? And Pryce? What were they doing on this ship? Philip could not remember. The commute between home and work was so short, and broken up by changing platforms to get from one train to another, that it was usually filled with unfinished stories and Philip always had to spend some time picking up the thread where he had left it on the last commuting stint. He browsed the previous pages and glanced over the text to reacquaint himself with Mrs. Hamlyn and Pryce. Gradually, the characters and setting came to life and he was ready to continue reading.

He had hardly finished the first paragraph when his attention was interrupted by a phone starting to ring. Philip lifted his head and kept still like a dog listening to footsteps in the distance. It was not his mobile so he turned his attention back to the story. The phone kept ringing. He could not concentrate on reading and looked up again.

On a bench, diagonally opposite from where he was standing, a young woman sat holding a mobile in one hand and staring at the screen. The phone rang. The woman stared. "Stop ringing!" her facial expression seemed to shout at the phone. She looked paralyzed by fear. Fear of answering the phone. She just sat there staring while the phone kept ringing. Why did she not answer? Was she hiding from someone? From her husband? Her mother? Her boss? The authorities?

At last, the phone stopped ringing. The young woman lowered the mobile to her lap, closed her eyes, and leaned back with her head against the window. She took a deep breath. She was relieved. Philip took a deep breath. He was relieved. He turned his attention back to W. Somerset Maugham, Mrs. Hamlyn, and Pryce.

"She doesn't like dogs!" said neither Mrs. Hamlyn nor Pryce as they passed each other on the deck, but a young man who had entered the train at the Arc de Triomf station.

"Seriously?" asked the young man's companion. "How do you know?"

"I just asked her. Just like that."

"That's great news, man! You think it has a future then?"

"Don't know. I mean. There's hope. I mean, with the dog question out of the way and all that."

The men moved to a pair of empty seats that had become available and Philip returned to Mrs. Hamlyn and Pryce. Finally he could get on with his story and make some headway into the plot.

★ ★ ★ ★ ★

The train arrived at the Urquinaona station. Philip packed W. Somerset Maugham into his backpack and stepped out onto the platform. He left his fellow travelers behind with their unfinished stories. It was time to move on—change the scene—and head for the next platform. Toward new travel companions with their unfinished stories. He with his own unfinished stories.

GAME

I sat down at a table with a good view of the big television where they would broadcast the game. I had plenty of choices for seating since the restaurant was empty. I looked at my watch. It was eight o'clock. I would have to wait forty-five minutes until the game would kick off.

I reached for the menu and flipped through the pages. I had already made up my mind about what I wanted to have—the same plate I always had. I was just killing time by looking at the establishment's complete offerings. If only I had taken a printout of the paper I was working on at the moment, then I could have used the time to read through a section or two. It would have been ideal since the deadline for submission was approaching rapidly.

"A shawarma plate and a beer, please," I said to the waiter who came over to the table to take my order as soon as I put down the menu.

★ ★ ★ ★ ★

A breeze of cold air passed through the restaurant when the front door opened into the unusually cold February evening. I looked up and watched a woman enter. She was wearing a long black coat and blue jeans that reached down to the floor with the hems torn at the heels of brown hiking boots. On her head she wore a purple cap; a brown scarf was wrapped around her neck, and her purple mittens matched the color of the cap. She was obviously coming from the Laundromat as she was carrying two giant plastic bags that appeared stuffed with clothes.

She laid down the bags, took off her mittens, and put them into her coat pockets. She glanced over the dining hall, unbuttoning her coat and loosening the scarf, revealing a thick brown sweater. She took off her cap and untucked her long black hair from under the coat collar. She met my gaze, smiled, and walked over to my table.

"Is this seat free?" she asked in English with a North American accent, pointing to the chair opposite to mine.

"Yes," I replied, wondering why she would choose to sit at my table when there were plenty of other seats available.

"Good," she said, smiling. "I don't want to take an entire table just for myself."

"Fair enough," I replied, even if I was not completely convinced by the argument. "It makes sense to use the space efficiently, especially when a Champions League game is coming up."

The waiter came to the table with my beer and the woman asked for a bottle of water.

"So you're here for the game?" she asked when the waiter had taken her order.

"Yes," I replied, unconsciously glancing at my wristwatch.

"It's still a bit early, isn't it?"

"Yes," I admitted, putting up an awkward smile. "I always make the same mistake, worry about not finding a good seat, rush to the restaurant, and end up way too early."

"A dedicated soccer fan?"

"No, not really. I don't watch that much. The big games. Against Madrid. The Champions League. You? A big Barça fan?"

"Can't say I am. I'm here mostly for the mood. I like the heated atmosphere of crowded scenes where a large group of people watches an exciting soccer match. These days I'm attracted to warm places."

The waiter came back to the table, bringing the bottle of water and my shawarma plate.

"Cheers!" the woman said after pouring herself a glass of water. "What's your name?"

"Cheers!" I replied, lifting my beer glass. "I'm Borgar."

"A what?"

"Borgar. B-O-R-G-A-R."

"Burger?"

"More or less. You can also call me Bob."

"Nice to meet you... Bob. I'm Alice. Where are you from?"

"Iceland."

"Awesome! I love Iceland. In a way. I definitely want to go there one day. A friend of mine went there a couple years ago and she showed me like a million photos when she came back. I was blown away by the landscape. So empty, yet so beautiful. It has a kind of outer space feel to it. So outer space that I heard

NASA is staging their Mars stimulation there. Is that true?”

“That’s true,” I said without actually having a clue whether it was really true, but pleased that it set one of my favorite jokes up. “I heard the premise is that if they manage to find intelligent life forms in Iceland, they could be hopeful the same holds for Mars.”

“Right!” the woman said, smiling. It seemed that my joke was at least a partial success. “In any case, intelligent life forms aside, it sounds like it’s a truly amazing and unique place.”

“Yeah, it’s a nice place for tourism. Totally different from what you get in Europe.”

“But Iceland belongs to Europe, doesn’t it?”

“Yes and no. Geographically speaking it’s half in Europe and half in North America, because it’s on the Atlantic Ridge. Genealogically we are predominantly of Norwegian origin with a few Celtic chromosomes thrown into the mix. Historically we belong to Europe through the connection with the Scandinavian dynasties. Culturally we are however a mixture between Europe and North America. There’s a lot of influence from the US in our lifestyle.”

“Oh yeah? How so?”

“Don’t know. Maybe because when Europe had its golden age, Icelanders were just poor farmers living in turf houses. Our golden age started only with the

Marshall Plan aid following the Second World War. We rose from poverty to riches under protection from the States. Iceland was an important strategic location in the Cold War. The US had an airbase there and poured money into the economy. I guess that explains to some extent why there's a lot of cultural influence from the US."

"I think that's the first time I've heard a European mention the States and culture in the same sentence. But what do you consider yourself? A European or an American?"

"Neither, really. I guess I associate with being Icelandic. But mostly I just consider myself, myself."

"Fair enough. And what brought you all the way to Barcelona? Escaping from the North American lifestyle? Trying to find your European roots?"

"No, not quite. I came here for a job. I work for a North American multinational company that has its European research arm based here. I'm an economist. Working mostly on game theory."

"Game theory? As in soccer?"

"No, not quite. Game theory as a formalism for studying decision making. It's used to model conflicts and cooperation between rational agents—as if they were playing a game. And you? What brought you over the Atlantic? Judging by your accent, I'm assuming you're American."

"Yes and no. I guess I can label myself as American. I'm originally from Canada but the desire for adventure drove me away from home and brought me all over the world. Compared to your game theory, my life is a completely different ball game. No fancy degree. Working odd jobs. Bars, restaurants, that sort of thing."

"Traveling all over the world doesn't sound that bad. Whereabouts?"

"All over, really. I've lived in the States, Argentina, Australia, London, Paris, Prague, Monaco, and now in Barcelona."

"That's quite an impressive list! And now, working in a Barcelona bar or restaurant?"

"No, not at the moment. I'm between jobs, as they say. I'm unemployed."

"And how do you fancy Barça's chances tonight?" the TV commentator asked their special guest as the waiter cranked up the volume and the pregame broadcast began. "They haven't been at the top of their game lately."

We let the television volume disrupt our conversation and started following the program. Gradually, people had begun to pour into the restaurant to watch the game, and Alice got the warm atmosphere she was seeking.

During the game and halftime we talked casually about the game and football in general. I ordered a couple more beers but Alice stuck with water.

The referee blew the final whistle and the crowd clapped. Barça had won and was in a good position to reach the next round of the competition. The waiter put the check on the table and I took out my card to pay. Alice took some coins from her pocket and started counting.

"Allow me," I said. "It was only a couple bottles of water. I'll take care of it."

We put our coats on while the waiter went to get the payment machine to process my card.

"You live close by?" I asked. "We could walk together if we're going in the same direction."

I had enjoyed Alice's company during the game and wanted to prolong it a few moments longer, although I did not have much time to spare due to the upcoming paper deadline. I thought it would be nice to walk together, exchange phone numbers, and then meet again for drinks or something when there was less time pressure.

"No, I can't really say I live close by," Alice replied, looking out the window. "Last night I slept in that bank lobby across the street. At the moment I'm homeless."

I looked at Alice. I looked at her bags. Perhaps she had not come directly from the Laundromat after all. I looked out the window, toward the bank across the street.

"Could you enter your pin, please?" the waiter asked, having returned with the payment machine.

I typed in the code and waited for the receipt before turning my attention back to Alice.

"Can I ask you a favor?" she asked as I put my card into my wallet.

"I suppose," I said, still shaken after what I had just heard.

"Can I crash on your couch tonight?"

Crash on my couch tonight? I hesitated. A few moments ago she had been an interesting woman I would have liked to get to know better. A few moments ago I would not have thought twice about inviting her to my place. Now, there was something holding me back. I felt awkward about inviting a homeless stranger to spend the night at my place.

"Just for one night," Alice begged. "I just want to get one night away from the cold. I want to sleep in a secure place. Away from the dangers of the street."

I felt my palms sweating and my cheeks burning as blood rushed to my head. I was very bad at handling spontaneous decisions. I always panicked. But now I needed to calm myself. I needed to think straight. To reason. I needed to put the situation into a context I was familiar with. I had to look at it from a game-theory perspective. I could set it up as a two-person game, where it was my turn to play. In that situation, I could either answer her request with a yes or a no. Then it would be her turn to show her cards. There were two possible outcomes. She could be honest or dishonest. Hence, in total, there were four possible results. If I said yes and she was dishonest, I would lose. If I said no and she was honest, she would lose. If I said yes and she was honest, we would both win. If I said no and she was dishonest, I would win. It was my turn to play. In game-theory terms the choice was clear, at least for a risk-averse person like me. In order to guarantee that I would not lose, my safest strategy would be to say no.

"I suppose you can," I replied, somewhat to my surprise. My gut feeling had overcome my reason. I was not behaving like the rational agents I wrote about in my academic papers.

"Thanks!" Alice exclaimed and hugged me. "I appreciate it very much."

She picked up her bags and we headed for the exit. I held the door open for her as we left the restaurant.

"I love Barcelona nights," Alice said as we hit the street. "And especially Gràcia. It's so busy and yet has such a calm atmosphere. It has a natural flow to it somehow. In a sense it's a bit like Icelandic landscapes, I guess, busy with exotic landforms but still so empty and quiet."

"Yes," I replied, not paying much attention to what she was saying. Had I made a mistake by following my gut feeling rather than my game-theory argumentation? She seemed like a nice girl and if I looked at the situation from a probabilistic perspective, there was no reason to worry. In all likelihood she was an honest person and I had no grounds to feel uneasy.

"Is that what you like about the Gràcia neighborhood?" Alice asked as we walked along Carrer de Verdi. "That it flows naturally like the Icelandic landscape?"

"I suppose," I said, wondering whether it was stupid of me to look at the situation from a probabilistic angle. Could I really claim that she was a nice and honest girl in all likelihood? I should assign some of the probability mass to the scenario where she was dishonest. What would happen then?

★ ★ ★ ★ ★

"This is it," I said as I fumbled with opening the door to my apartment.

We entered and I locked the door behind us with the bolt. I thought about locking it with a key as well—to bar Alice from running away with my belongings. That might look awkward, though. How would I justify my actions if she asked?

"Here's the bedroom, the study, the bathroom," I said, leading Alice toward the living room. "And the kitchen is farther down the hall."

"It's a nice place you've got," Alice said as we entered the living room. "You must be making a small fortune playing this game thing of yours."

"That'll be your bed tonight," I said, pulling the seat of the sofa forward to turn it into a bed. "Let me get you some sheets."

I went into the study and grabbed a set of bedsheets from the wardrobe that covered one wall of the room opposite a densely packed bookshelf. I took a deep breath. Alice looked to be a perfectly harmless woman. There was definitely no reason for me to worry about her being in my apartment.

"Good night," I said after preparing the sofa bed for Alice.

"I hope you get a nice deep sleep," Alice replied, smiling.

I replied with an awkward smile and left the living room, heading over to my bedroom.

★ ★ ★ ★ ★

I opened my eyes and looked at the alarm clock. It was one a.m. I could not sleep.

"I hope you get a nice deep sleep," Alice had said. "You must be making a small fortune playing this game thing of yours."

What did she mean by that? A nice deep sleep? Was she hoping I would be so deeply asleep that she would have a good opportunity to rob me while I snored? Was she eyeing my laptop? My camera? My stereo?

I took a deep breath. There was nothing to be afraid of. Probability was on my side. In all likelihood Alice was an honest woman. She was here as my guest, just to get a secure night's sleep. She was not here to cause me harm.

★ ★ ★ ★ ★

I opened my eyes and looked at the alarm clock. It was two a.m. I held my breath, listening to the sounds coming from the living room. There was a deep breathing sound. Like someone in a good sleep.

"I want to sleep in a secure place. Away from the dangers of the street," she had said when convincing me to take her to my place for the night.

How could she feel secure while sleeping at a stranger's place? How did she know I was no danger to her? I could just as well be a lunatic, violent, and a rapist. Was she secure because she had a third party on her side? Someone who she would let in during the night while I was fast asleep? Or in a deep sleep, as she had put it. Was she pretending to be asleep? Was she waiting for me to fall asleep? Waiting until she would have the apartment to herself? Waiting until she could have her way and rob me? I should have locked the door with the key.

★ ★ ★ ★ ★

I opened my eyes and looked at the alarm clock. It was three a.m. I heard noise coming from the hall outside the apartment. I heard the rattling of metal. I cuddled up in the fetal position, hugging my extra pillow. What had I done? What was going to happen? I was such an idiot. Why had I let that woman into my house? What would I do?

I heard my neighbor's door open. He was most likely coming home from a late-night shift. The danger was over for the time being, but my heart kept pounding at an accelerated rate. My mind replayed a series of scenes in my head, over and over again. The moment when Alice walked into the restaurant. How she singled me out as her victim. The scene when we walked together through the streets of Gràcia. How she smiled a seemingly innocent smile when saying good night.

★ ★ ★ ★ ★

I opened my eyes and looked at the alarm clock. It was four a.m. I heard someone clear their throat by the foot of the bed. It was Alice. She stood there looking at me with her hands behind her back.

"Awake, are we?" Alice asked, grinning. "Having problems sleeping because you didn't dare lock the front door with a key? Who do you take me for? Some evil bitch who's going to do you harm while you sleep?"

I blinked, but I could not utter a word. My head felt heavy, halfway between being asleep and awake.

"Alice!" someone shouted from the hallway. "Let's go!"

I felt a knot in my stomach. I wanted to jump out of bed but I could not move. It was as if my arms were tied to my body and my legs to each other.

"Shh," Alice whispered, pulling one hand from behind her back and bringing her index finger to her lips. "Just lie back and relax. I'm leaving."

She pulled the other hand from behind her back and pointed a gun in my face.

"Game over!" she yelled as she pulled the trigger and everything went black before my eyes.

★ ★ ★ ★ ★

I opened my eyes and looked at the alarm clock. It was ten a.m. I would be late for work. I had overslept.

I got out of bed and put on a pair of sweatpants and a T-shirt.

I staggered, half-asleep, into the hallway and to the bathroom. As I sat down on the toilet I started recalling last night's events. The game. Alice. The gun. Was she just a dream? Was she still sleeping? Was she real? Had she left? What was a dream and what was reality? Were my things in their place?

I looked around the bathroom. Everything seemed to be as it should be. No, wait. My hair dryer. My hair dryer was gone. Alice had stolen my hair dryer.

I walked back into the hallway and looked into the living room. The sofa bed had been turned back into a sofa. The bedsheets lay neatly folded with my hair dryer on top. Alice was nowhere to be seen.

I heard noise coming from the kitchen. The washing machine was going into its final and loudest spin. As I entered, I saw Alice standing by the stove flipping a pancake. She had changed clothes from the night before and was wearing black jeans and a red sweater.

"Good morning," she said, smiling. "How long you slept. I thought you were never going to wake up."

"Yes, no, good morning," I murmured, rubbing my right earlobe between my thumb and index finger. "I didn't sleep all that well. I had some weird nightmares."

"That's too bad," she said, frowning. "I hope you don't mind me borrowing one of your towels and taking a shower. I also took the liberty of using your washing machine to wash one load of clothes."

"No, that's fine. I don't mind."

"Very well," she said, rubbing her hands together. "Enough chitchat. Breakfast is ready. Could you take these into the living room?"

She handed me a large plate of thick American pancakes and two smaller plates with cutlery and napkins.

"Lungo or espresso?" she asked as a trained waitress. "Milk or sugar?"

"An espresso, thanks. Black," I said as I took the pancakes to the living room. In the background, I could hear the humming of my Nespresso machine thrusting hot water through the coffee capsule.

"Do you mind if I use your dryer while we have breakfast?" she asked as I reentered the kitchen, seeing her already taking her clothes from the washing machine and loading them into the dryer.

"Not at all," I said, yawning, not fully recovered from the disrupted sleep. "Is there anything more I can bring to the table?"

"Indeed!" Alice said, handing me a tray with a mug of coffee, my espresso cup, maple syrup, Nutella, two jars of jam and butter.

★ ★ ★ ★ ★

We sat down at the dining table. A breakfast like this had not been prepared in the house for a long time. I had forgotten I even had all this stuff in my cupboards.

"The pancakes are very tasty," I said, having taken the first bite. They were truly delicious and I could feel the energy slowly build up in my body.

"I'm glad you like them."

"It's nice to have a proper breakfast once in a while. I usually just have two or three cups of coffee until lunch."

We sat in silence for a while enjoying the pancakes and coffee.

"How did you end up on the streets?" I asked after having cleared some of the fog in my mind with a sip of my espresso.

"My home went away with my last job," Alice answered, pausing for a moment before continuing. "I was an assistant chef at a burger joint in Sants. I was living with the main chef. The relationship went up in flames. But it wasn't all my fault. I didn't know the deep fryer would catch fire when I threw that bottle."

"What bottle?" I asked, not sure if the story was confusing or if I was just tired.

"The bottle of whiskey I was unloading from a delivery box. I'd just found out that Tony, the Swedish chef, the chief burger flipper, the owner, the guy I was living with, had slept with big-boobs Barbie, the waitress who was apparently just as busy serving her massive melons as she was serving juicy burgers. That pretty much sums up how I ended up on the street. I threw the bottle. Tony's burger joint burned down. He threw me out."

"When was this?"

"A month ago or so."

"How long had you been working at Tony's?"

"Half a year."

"And before that?" I asked. "If you don't mind me asking."

"No, it's fine," she said and gave me a smile. "I owe you for the favor... Before that? I was working at a raw-food vegan tapas bar. The food was—believe it or not—really good, but it was hard to sell the tapas bar concept without the ham and cheese platters. The place went out of business... without flames... in many ways.

"Before that I was fired from a hotel receptionist position. For giving one of the guests an off-the-menu room service, if you know what I mean. All legal, but maybe not very professional."

"Wow, it seems like you're haunted by some sort of bad luck."

"I'm not sure if my systemic misfortune can be written off as bad luck. I'd rather say I have a talent for messing up everything I do."

★ ★ ★ ★ ★

After breakfast we took the plates to the kitchen and I washed them while Alice folded her laundry, which could hardly have been fully dried after such a short while in the dryer.

"Well, I shall be off then," she said as she took the final piece of clothing out of the dryer, folded it, and put it in her bag. "I don't want to keep you all day. You must need to get to work."

"Would you like to stay another night?" I asked her, putting aside the fork I had been drying. "Or at least stay for a while to finish your laundry, let it dry properly?"

"That's a very sweet offer, thank you," she said, walking over to me, putting a hand on my upper arm, and looking me in the eyes. "But I've made a principle of not staying at the same place for more than one night. I don't want to build habits. Not in my current situation. But thanks for the offer. I appreciate it. Maybe later. Under other circumstances. When I've managed to get myself off the street.

"Thanks for everything," she said as she leaned forward and kissed me on both cheeks. "Goodbye."

44

I walked her to the door. A tear formed in the corner of my eye as I watched her leave my apartment, walking into the hallway with a giant plastic bag in each hand. I swept the tear away just when she turned around to give me a smile before descending the stairs.

The Minister for Culture closes his eyes and puts on the virtual reality headset. When he opens his eyes again he finds himself standing on an Arctic ice field. An arrow-shaped wooden sign is anchored into the ground and engraved with the words *North Pole*. The minister's gaze follows the direction of the sign and stops on a white blob moving about on the ice, almost invisible against the white background. He uses the joystick to zoom in and get a better view of the thing and discovers that it is a polar bear—the king of the Arctic.

The minister admires the big and strong animal. He has a thing for predators. That is how he wants to be seen as a politician. He wants to be feared—and not only because his mother is an influential figure in the leadership of the party.

The bear keeps moving about on the glacier. It takes five steps forward, stops and swings its right front leg through the air as if to strike an imaginary tennis ball. It groans, turns around and walks five steps back to its original position. Turning around again, it takes five steps forward, stops, swings its right front leg through the air, groans, turns around, walks back...

The minister watches the polar bear walk back and forth several times, repeating the same act of swinging its front leg through the air, followed by a disturbing groan. He follows the animal, moving his head from the left to the right to the left to the right to the left to the right... as if he is following the swinging movement of a hypnotizer's pendulum... to the left to the right to the left to the right to the left... he feels his eyelids get heavier... to the left to the right to the left to the right...

"Take me away from here!" the minister suddenly shouts, turning away from the polar bear and bringing his palms to the headphones covering his ears as if he is trying to escape all awareness of the moaning animal.

The Minister for Culture finds himself floating up into the sky and flying slowly south across the globe, over Europe, across the Sahara Desert, and is dropped onto the eastern part of the African Continent.

The minister looks around the savanna. The hot sun is beating down on the grassland. Small and isolated trees and bushes are scattered around the horizon. In the distance, he spots a group of animals grazing on the dry pasture. He refreshes his elementary school geography—or was it biology—and guesses it is a herd of gazelles. Farther along the horizon he spots a big dotted cat quietly tiptoeing toward the gazelles. That animal he knows. He recognizes it without a doubt as a cheetah.

Suddenly, the cheetah jumps forward and starts running, only to come to an abrupt halt after a mere few meters, as if it has hit an invisible wall. It sits down biting its paw, looking toward the herd of gazelles. Finally, it stands up and casually trots back to its original spot where it lies down, resting its chin on its front paws, and a tear runs town its cheek.

The Minister for Culture takes off the virtual reality goggles and looks over to Yvette, the Chief Concept Designer of Studio Zero who is standing a few steps away with arms crossed over her chest, chin raised, and a proud smile across her face.

"What the hell is this?" cries the minister, holding up the virtual reality goggles and shaking them for extra emphasis. "What did I just see?"

"Well, this is what you asked us to do," Yvette replies, her smile fading into a serious look. "It's our initial concept for the Virtual Reality Zoo. As you most likely are aware, our brief was to create a virtual reality concept where people can explore animals in their natural environment but merge that experience with the most remarkable aspects of our long-standing cultural heritage of city zoos."

"I know very well what I asked for!" snaps the minister through clenched teeth. "This is *not* what I asked for."

The minister knows exactly what he asked for. He himself wrote the first draft of the brief, although the idea had been his mother's and he'd asked the younger staff at the ministry to finish the brief and add all the technology stuff.

"Can you elaborate?" asks Yvette.

"For example, why are the animals behaving so strangely? I do not remember asking for that. And that is because I did not ask for that."

"I see," Yvette says, smiling and nodding her head like a patient schoolteacher. "Let's take a step back.

Let me explain our approach in more detail. As you saw, we've followed the brief literally and taken the natural environment of the animals as a starting point and background scene in our application. As for the cultural heritage of city zoos, the brief was vague and lacking in detail so we had to choose which attributes we found the most striking. On one hand we have confined spaces and on the other hand we have chosen mental stress. Brought together, this means that all the animals appear to be in their natural environment but their movement is constrained by invisible cages. They're all stressed, nervous, and, quite frankly, demented to a greater or lesser degree—just as they are in our traditional city zoos all around the globe."

"Why on earth would anyone want to see virtual demented animals?" the minister shouts, emphasizing his words with a *mano a borsa* hand gesture he most probably learned from the *Godfather* movies, but is completely out of sync with his own personality.

"I'd guess for the same reason they go to see real demented animals in real zoos," Yvette answers calmly, placing her hands on her waist.

"But why demented?" the minister asks, slipping into a high-pitch squeal, as if he is going to cry.

"Well, the brief asked us to preserve the centuries-old cultural heritage of city zoos," Yvette answers, in an assertive voice. "After extensive research and internal discussion between our concept designers and anthropologists, we've come to the conclusion that this is best achieved by confined spaces and mental illnesses."

"No, no, no!" cries the minister. "That is not true! That is not what I wanted. I wanted... I wanted to see children petting... happy animals... kind and charismatic lion tamers... explorers... *That* is our cultural heritage... Confined spaces and mental illness... *That* is not culture! That is cruelty. That is just..."

The Minister for Culture does not finish the sentence but throws the virtual reality headset on the floor and storms out of the room, slamming the door behind him.

CHAIN OF LOVE

I opened my eyes and raised my seat back from a sleeping position to a laid-back position. Outside the window the sun was rising over the horizon, painting a pinkish layer over the light-blue background. We were driving along a highway, past a mixture of low- and mid-rise buildings—entering Buenos Aires, I guessed. I looked at my watch. It was just after six o'clock. If I remembered the schedule correctly, we had still a good hour's drive ahead of us before reaching Retiro station, which probably meant we had not yet reached Buenos Aires itself but were perhaps passing through some of its satellite towns.

The bus was mostly silent, apart from the low hum from the engine and the murmur from the friction between the tires and the tarmac, combined with occasional deep-sleep breathing and light snoring. I guessed most of the passengers were still asleep, making the most of the time before we reached our destination. I had slept like a log, had been tired after yesterday's walking and was knocked out almost immediately after finishing the champagne glass they served after dinner. I smiled at the thought. Until recently, bubbles and buses had not been associated ideas in my mind, but I was really enjoying the bed-bus concept of South America. I was surprised by the comfort and liking the option to step on a bus in the evening in one town and wake up the next morning in another location, hundreds of kilometers away. Going from one thing to another was exactly what I needed at the moment. At the end of a fifteen-year-long relationship and on a ten-year work anniversary, I needed a few weeks of distraction in my life to break up my habits and bridge the gap toward a new beginning. It was a turbulent ride, though. My spirit was constantly oscillating between ups and downs.

★ ★ ★ ★ ★

"Awake?" a young girl whispered, her head barely reaching over the headrest of the seat in front of me.

"Yes," I replied. "The morning sun woke me up."

"I just woke up because I didn't want to sleep anymore... but I didn't wake my mommy. I'm a good girl. I can wake up on my own and allow Mommy to sleep."

"That's good," I said, yawning. Even if I was technically awake and well rested, my brain was not yet firing on all cylinders.

"That's how I make the chain of love longer."

"Huh?" I asked, gradually waking up. "Chain of love? What's that?"

"It's a chain of being good," the girl whispered, inching her head a little higher over the seat back. "My daddy's boss allowed him to go home early yesterday. Daddy read a story to Javi. Javi is my little brother. Javi gave me a big hug before we got on the bus. I allow Mommy to sleep and she will be kind to somebody today. That somebody will be kind to somebody else. Then the chain of love will go all over the world and end all wars and pain."

"Interesting," I said, nodding my head. "All wars will end just because your daddy's boss allowed him to go home early yesterday?"

"Yes," the girl replied without a hint of hesitation. "And because Mommy taught us to make the chain longer."

"Nice! I like that. But what happens if someone breaks the chain?"

"Uh..." The girl placed an index finger on her chin and paused for a moment before continuing. "No problem. Just start it again."

"Impressive!" A chain of charitable acts that spreads through the world and rids it of misery and acts of cruelty. Now, there was a concept I really liked.

"Where you coming from?" the girl asked, changing the subject.

"Iguazú."

"What were you doing in Iguazú?"

"Exploring the waterfalls and the power plant."

"All alone?"

"Yes."

"You're not sad because you have no one to talk to?"

"I have people to talk to. I talk to other guests at the places where I'm staying."

"Are they also on the bus?"

"Who?"

"The other guests."

"No. Some left earlier. Some were leaving later. Some were traveling to other destinations."

"What did you talk about?"

"This and that. Where we were from. Our jobs. Our travels. There was this one couple at the hotel in Iguazú who had an exciting cruise coming up. They were going to sail on the Southern Ocean around Antarctica, and we talked about their plans."

"Going with them on the cruise?"

"No."

"Where you going?"

"Buenos Aires."

"Why?"

"See the city and visit an acquaintance."

"What's an acquaintance?"

"Someone you know a little but not really well. In this case, someone I've met a few times at conferences."

"What's a conferences?"

"An event where people get together and talk about their work."

"Going to stay with him?"

"Yes."

"What's his name?"

"Matteo."

"Is he your friend?"

"Well..." I took a peek out the window as if I expected to find the right answer along the highway. "Yes and no. We've met a couple of times. Went out to dinner and drinks with other people from the conference. Not sure if he qualifies as a friend, though."

"He's stranger?"

"No..." I hesitated, again consulting the highway outside the window. "Not really... either... I guess."

"Good," the girl said with such a serious expression that I got the feeling I was being lectured. "You shouldn't talk to strangers."

"María," came a female voice from the row of seats in front of me. "Who are you talking to?"

"The man behind us," the girl whispered back, sitting down in her seat and disappearing from my view. "He's alone but not sad."

"You remember what I said about talking to strangers?"

"Yes, Mommy... but I started."

"In that case..." the woman whispered to María before turning in her seat to face me. "I hope she didn't disturb you."

"Not at all," I replied, smiling. "I enjoyed the company."

"Very good," the woman said, turning back in her seat.

The mother and daughter continued whispering and I returned to admiring the view outside the bus window. It looked as if we had finally entered Buenos Aires. We drove past densely populated areas and

I watched the buildings pass by without trying to pay them any special attention. I enjoyed letting the surroundings get sucked into my subconscious without thinking too much. That was one thing I had vowed to do before setting off on my trip through South America. I tried to plan ahead as little as possible and let myself drift, following the direction of the wind. There was nothing I necessarily needed to see, no place demanded visiting, no photo had to be taken, there was nothing I was absolutely required to remember. I had decided I needed two months in a foreign environment to clear my head of the life expectations I had consciously and unconsciously constructed through the years. Upon returning to Barcelona, reality would kick in again. I would have to build a new daily routine—a life without Mercè. Also, I felt I should decide if it was time for a career change after ten years at the university. Change into a softer line of work, perhaps—something less computational. Maybe something where I could apply my joy of creative writing. Not that I had any idea what that could be.

However, that was something to think about later. For now I had to attend to what was happening in my immediate surroundings. The bus had stopped at what seemed to be a fairly big bus station. The crew made no announcement about where we were and I couldn't see any signs with station names. Most, if not all, of the passengers were preparing to step off the bus. I looked at my watch and browsed the bus schedule. According to the schedule, we still had half an hour to go before we would arrive at the Retiro station in Buenos Aires.

"This is Retiro," said a woman who was obviously able to read my mind or gestures. "We're ahead of schedule."

I looked up. María and her mother were standing in the walkway between the rows of seats, ready to leave the bus.

"Enjoy your stay in Buenos Aires," the mother continued before leading her daughter by the hand down the aisle.

"Bye, stranger," María said and winked.

"Bye, thanks," I replied, watching as they made their way toward the exit.

I picked up the linen bag I used to hold my most valuable and essential possessions and stepped off the bus together with the last group of passengers.

★ ★ ★ ★ ★

After collecting my backpack from the luggage compartment, it was time to head into the city center. I knew the main square was east of Retiro, but upon stepping through the station doors I realized I had no idea through which entrance I was exiting, nor did I know which direction would take me east.

60

I stopped for a moment and looked over the surroundings. The streets were waking up. There wasn't a big crowd of people outside the station but a few merchants were setting up their stalls and an occasional passer-by made their way past the merchandise. By the looks of it, it did not seem as if I had left through the main entrance.

I walked down the ramp from the station and into the street. I turned right and followed the station wall, carefully taking mental note of signs with street names. After a couple of blocks I turned right without hesitating, again being careful to remember the street name. I walked to the next crossing, crossed the street, and turned back. I crossed another street, turned left, and walked over to a bench in a park adjacent to the station, directly across the street from where I had exited.

When traveling in unknown places I didn't like looking at a map while standing or walking in the middle of a street. I didn't want to draw attention to myself as the proverbial lost tourist. I felt like it made me vulnerable to mugging and tricking.

I took off my backpack, sat down on the bench, and picked up my Lonely Planet guide to South America. Normally I would have searched for a café before consulting the travel guide but on my short walk around the station, I had not encountered any. Maybe I had been too occupied with remembering street names.

I looked at the map of the Retiro area and started locating myself using the street names I had noted in my mental notebook. I was pleased to find out that a single street would take me directly to the center, where I wanted to go. Albeit a decent walk, it was a straight and easy route. I just had to follow San Martín and it would take me straight to Plaza de Mayo. As it turned out, the walk was straight south rather than east as I had for some reason mistakenly thought.

★ ★ ★ ★ ★

I entered the center at the northwestern corner of Plaza de Mayo. It was still fairly early in the morning and I had plenty of time to kill before getting in touch with Matteo, my acquaintance. Or was he my friend? Or a stranger? In any case, it was still too early to call. In fact, I was unsure of when there would be a good time to contact him. It was a Saturday morning and I had no idea about his weekend routine, or the local etiquette relating to pre-lunch phone calls.

I started my exploration of the city center by walking down to the Casa Rosada and back. Then I threaded the streets around Plaza de Mayo, looking at nothing in particular but drinking in everything at the same time. I walked past a newsagent who was opening his shop. I went in and bought a map of the city. I reasoned that when looking for Matteo's place it would be better to have a detailed map rather than the spotty sketches in the Lonely Planet guide. In particular since I blamed it for this morning's confusion between east and south. It's not you who is messed up, I said to myself, it's the travel guide's fault.

After circling the streets around Plaza de Mayo for almost an hour, I came across a café that looked inviting. I had not been looking for a place to sit down but realized the walk through the center had stimulated my appetite and thought it might be a good idea to have some breakfast and explore my new map to try to get oriented. I ordered a cappuccino and a croissant, unfolded the map, and made my initial attempt at locating Matteo's place. With the map spread out in front of me on the table, I realized I was faced with an enormous city and a single street name. I had practically nothing in my hands to narrow down the search. Needles and haystacks came to mind. Neither did I know anything about the neighborhoods of the city nor did I know in which neighborhood Matteo lived, or whether his address was in the center or suburbs, north, south, east, or west. I tried to scan the map from the top left to the bottom right, but soon recognized this would take ages. Then I took a look at semi-random points around the center and read the street names in the vicinity, in the hope of finding Olavarría. Neither approach was successful. For a moment I regretted having left my smartphone behind in Spain. Finding the address would have been so easy with a proper phone and a data plan.

I had decided to leave my smartphone behind in order to cut all connections with the old world during the two months I planned to spend exploring the new world. I had decided to take a break from the digital world and live an analog life for a few weeks. There were more things in life than algorithms, I convinced myself, not everything needed to be calculated. Yet I did struggle with trying to live my life less algorithmically. It was just the way I thought.

Without having found what I was looking for, I folded the map and finished my breakfast. It was still relatively early in the morning and I wondered if it was now late enough to call Matteo. It was half past nine and I reasoned it would probably not be decent to call him until ten. However, I had hardly finished that thought when my old not-so-smart-phone started ringing.

"Hi, it's Matteo. How are you? Have you arrived in Buenos Aires yet?"

"Yes, I arrived on a bus early in the morning. I've just finished my breakfast."

"Very good. Where are you?"

"Close to Plaza de Mayo, I think, I seem to be quite without a sense of directions today."

"No worries. That's a perfect location. It's very easy to get to my place from there. Go down toward Casa Rosada, stay on the right side, and take bus 64 heading for La Boca. The bus will turn south and go past San Telmo, then under a bridge and past a park on your right. Then the bus will turn left into La Boca. You should get off before it turns right again, at Puente Nicolás Avellaneda. Then walk back a block and a half and turn left into Olavarría. My place will be on the right, above a pharmacy. Got it?"

"Yes. I think so. Casa Rosada, right side, bus 64 to La Boca, south, San Telmo, bridge, park, left, get off before it turns right and then back, left into Olavarría, and a pharmacy."

"Exactly! See you in a bit."

"Okay, bye."

I repeated the directions in my head. Casa Rosada, right side, bus 64 to La Boca, bridge, park, left, get off before it turns right, and then above a pharmacy. That didn't sound that hard.

I paid my bill and headed across Plaza de Mayo toward Casa Rosada, reminding myself of the first part of the route, bus 64 toward La Boca. As I came to the bus stop, bus 64 to La Boca was arriving and I hopped on.

Once on the bus I asked the driver how much the ride cost. He pointed me to a machine further down the aisle. I walked to the machine and read the instructions. It turned out I had two options to pay the fare. I could either pay one peso with a transport card or two pesos with a two-peso coin. I had neither. I only had a two-peso bill.

"Can I pay with a two-peso bill?" I asked the driver.

"No."

"Do you have change for a bill to coin?" I asked, even if it was practically the same question as before.

"No."

I stood for a moment and contemplated my options. The bus had already started moving so getting off to look for change was not an option. On the other hand, I felt bad about just sitting down without paying.

"I'll take it."

A man in a blue uniform walked toward the ticket machine and paid my ride with his transport card.

"Thank you very much," I said, handing him my two-peso bill.

"I paid only one peso with my card and I don't have any change."

"That's no problem," I said, extending the two-peso bill toward him. "My ride was going to cost me two pesos anyway."

"Don't worry about it," the man said, holding his hands up, as if he was surrendering to someone assaulting him with a weapon.

"No, please, take it," I insisted. "It's the least I can offer."

The worker shook his head, smiling, and returned to his seat. I thanked him again for the favor and found myself a window seat farther back. I felt awkward accepting the man's help. I was pretty sure my liquidity was better than his and the two-peso bill would be of better use in his hands than mine. I wondered how I could pay him back. I would have liked to do him a favor someday, somehow. However, it was unlikely that our paths would cross ever again. On that thought, my mind wandered to Mercè. Would our paths cross again? It seemed impossible they wouldn't, yet it was hard to imagine how that encounter would play out, given all that had happened, given all that was said, given all that had been shouted.

When the bus stopped at the next station, the two passengers sitting in front of me stood up and left. A woman and a little girl. Just before stepping off the bus, the girl turned around, faced me with a smile and waved. I was taken aback. It was my new friend María.

Before I could wave back, the door had already closed behind them and the bus started moving.

Was this some sort of a sign? Was my episode with the worker just one link in the chain of love? Maybe María's mother had been kind to this man and he had played his part in the chain by paying my fare. Now it was my turn to be kind to someone. My turn to extend the chain of love that would eventually end all wars and misery of this world. Perhaps the man was not a part of the chain that had started when María's father's boss had given him half a day off. The man could equally be a part of a different chain of love, a different thread but weaving the same fabric of kindness that spreads over the world and safeguards us all. I shook my head and decided that was enough lyric prose for the time being, I had a place to get to.

I looked out the window and tried to remember Matteo's description of the route. Bus 64, park, get off before it turns right. That was about all I could remember. How on earth was I going to know when to get off?

I took out my map and unfolded it as much as the limited space on the bus allowed. Now that I had the name of the neighborhood I should be able to perform a more effective search for Matteo's address. My eyes wandered over the map and quickly traced the route of the crow's flight from Casa Rosada, over San Telmo to the La Boca neighborhood, and then zoomed in to search for Olavarría. Bingo. There it was. I moved my gaze back toward Casa Rosada and tried to replay Matteo's description on the map. Turn south and pass under a bridge. I looked out the window and saw we were approaching a highway overpass. I went back to the map and found the park and the left turn into La Boca. It was all coming back to me. Now I only had to get off before the bus turned right, after having turned left. I looked back out the window. The overpass was behind us and the park was on our right. Soon the bus took a left turn. Everything was under control and it would be a piece of cake to find the right place to get off.

I started listening to the names of the stations and tried to locate them on the map to make sure I got out at the right one. At first I struggled. I was too slow in my scanning. Gradually I got the hang of it, though, keeping my index finger on the map, listening and looking out the window. But, just as I had developed the system I was so captured by the view that I decided it was much more interesting to observe the surroundings of this unfamiliar city than to track the bus journey on a map. In fact, it was really not that difficult to know where I should get off. All I had to do was to wait for the bus to turn right. Then I would know I had missed my stop but was at least in the right neighborhood. I could worry later about finding the right house. So I removed my finger from the map, stopped listening to bus stop names, and enjoyed the view.

Eventually, the bus turned right and I rang the bell and got off at the first opportunity. I looked around to familiarize myself with my surroundings. On the other side of the street there was a promenade that ran along a canal. On my side, there was a row of run-down buildings. For a moment I thought I remembered some stories about La Boca not being the safest place in the city. Maybe it had not been a good idea to deviate from the scripted route. Despite my worries about this not being a place for a public display of disorientation, I sat down on the bus stop bench and looked at the map to try to find my exact location relative to where Matteo lived.

"Looking for something?"

My heart jumped and I fastened my grip on the map and pressed my knees together to secure my backpack. I looked up and saw an elderly man sit down beside me.

"I'm looking for Olavarría," I admitted.

"Olavarría," the man said slowly. "Continue on this street until the next intersection, then turn right and Olavarría will be the third street you cross."

"Thank you very much!"

I put the map into my backpack and followed the old man's directions with mixed feelings and slightly worried about whether he was sending me in the right direction or leading me astray. However, in an instant I was standing in front of the pharmacy Matteo had described to me over the phone. Now, it seemed I owed two acts of kindness to the chain of love.

★ ★ ★ ★ ★

After walking around in San Telmo for over forty minutes looking for a place to have lunch, I was glad to finally see a café that looked promising. La Poesía. Although I claimed to be a man of prose I decided to drop in. I had passed several nice-looking places on my morning stroll, but upon entering each one I had found something that turned me off. Too empty. Too crowded. Too bright. Too dark. I didn't have clear criteria for what I wanted in a place, but for some reason, when it came to making a decision, I found it easy to speculate that around the corner the grass might be greener, the furniture might be browner, or the food might be tastier. I did that every so often when I was deliberately looking for a place. I walked until I was too hungry to continue. Then I finally entered whichever place was closest to my point of desperation and I usually ended up eating at places that were much inferior to the ones I had passed but

71

discarded. I was glad that this seemed not to be the case with La Poesía. Could it be that for once my indecision had paid off?

La Poesía had a mountain hut look to it. The tables and chairs were made of wood, old but stylish. The walls were covered with black-and-white pictures and artifacts from the past. Despite being antique, the café had a fresh atmosphere, the interior seemed carefully curated, and every item was in the right place while not seeming artificially staged. The place looked naturally charming.

The café was about half full. The patrons spanned a wide range of ages and appearances. By the front door were two elderly men engaged in a lively discussion. On their table lay a pile of worn-out books. I could not hear their conversation, but I imagined they were book critics arguing about the literary value of some old classic. Toward the back was a group of teenage girls chatting while glancing at their mobiles. In between there was a woman in her midthirties—I guessed— typing away on her laptop, latte on one side and a notebook on the other.

I found myself a table in the middle of the café and sat down. Again, I reminded myself of how lucky I had been with being picky about the place to have lunch today. If I hadn't been, I would probably have missed this one. There was something about this café I would have been sorry to miss.

I ordered myself a steak sandwich and a beer. It was my third day in Buenos Aires and I had not yet had a steak sandwich. Over breakfast this morning, Matteo had recommended I gave it a try. Himself being a vegetarian, it may have sounded a curious suggestion, but entirely consistent with the character of the man who I was now in no doubt of calling a friend, rather than an acquaintance or a stranger. He had an ear for listening out for what I generally enjoyed and then provided tailor-made recommendations using his local knowledge of the city.

While I waited for my food, I picked up my notebook and started writing my travel log for Buenos Aires. It wasn't very much of a travel log, though. It was just a log—a collection of random, or at least pseudorandom, thoughts about everything and nothing. I hadn't done much, in the touristy sense, that is. I hadn't done all the essential things I should have done according to Lonely Planet. I had just walked around aimlessly, thinking and observing the life of the city, occasionally sitting down for a while, jotting some well-chosen words in my notebook. I had been able to relax and get over my initial paranoia about safety in the city. My writing was fluent and I felt better than I had done in a long time. My time away from home was doing me good. My spirit was definitely being lifted. I didn't feel bad about not experiencing the city as most tourists did. Instead, I was experiencing the city in my own way. I'm a thinker, I wrote in my notebook, and if a city encourages me to think, I think. I'm a walker, and if a city encourages me to walk, I walk. I'm a writer—in a liberal sense of the word—and if a city encourages me to write, I write. Even in Buenos Aires, I don't need to learn how to dance tango as long as I have my pen dancing across the paper.

Between sentences I looked up from my notebook and across the café, to the bar, drinking in the atmosphere of the place, and not least of all to steal a peek at the waitresses who I found very beautiful. After a fifteen-year-long relationship with Mercè I felt like I was for the first time in a long time paying attention to beautiful women—consciously, at least. If only Mercè had had the same monogamous vision of our relationship, then there would have been no Fábian, no explosive revelation, and no breakup. On the other hand, there would have been no trip through South America, no revitalizing stroll through Buenos Aires, and no new adventures. Maybe the whole thing was turning out to be liberating for me rather than humiliating.

It was at the end of one of those glances, and when I was about to return to my writings, that I recognized a familiar person standing at the bar talking to one of the waitresses. If I was not mistaken it was Ellen, a Canadian woman I had met over breakfast in Iguazú a few days earlier. I had had an interesting chat with her and her husband.

"Hey, what a coincidence to see you here!" I said as I walked up to the bar and greeted Ellen.

"You here! How nice! You speak Spanish, right?" Ellen asked and sighed. "I want to order a steak sandwich to take with me on the bus to Bariloche but I don't seem to be able to get across that I want the sandwich as a takeaway."

"No worries," I said and turned to the waitress. *"Quiere el lomito para llevar."*

"Ah, para llevar, ahora sí," answered the waitress, smiling with relief. *"¿Lo quiere completo?"*

"You want the complete sandwich?"

"What's complete?"

"With ham, fried egg, cheese, bacon..."

"No, just the plain steak sandwich," Ellen replied. "I remember having one when I was in Buenos Aires twelve years ago. It was delicious."

"Solo el sandwich," I translated to the waitress but decided to leave out the latter part as I judged it irrelevant to the order. I continued my job as an interpreter, translating the last part of the business exchange involving the payment.

"Why don't we go over to my table while you wait for your food," I said and pointed toward the space where I had installed myself. "I'm waiting for my own sandwich."

As we waited, we recounted our adventures since we had last seen each other in Iguazú. Time flew by and before we knew it our sandwiches had arrived.

"I'll have to go now," Ellen said. "I cannot be late for the bus."

"Well, enjoy Bariloche, and your cruise, and your sandwich. Not necessarily in that order."

"Thanks for stepping in to save the order. If only I could repay you somehow."

"There's no need for reimbursement. I'm just extending the chain of love. You don't owe me anything. I just deposited an act of kindness into the universal world bank of love. You can do the same by helping someone else. We can then make withdrawals when we need them. We don't need to pay back favors in a reciprocal manner. We just need to keep being nice to each other in order to keep the bank liquid."

"What?"

"Never mind," I replied, smiling. "Some other time. Go catch your bus."

My contribution to the chain of love had been quite small. No lifesaving acts of heroism. Nevertheless, it made me feel good to be finally part of the chain that would eventually spread all over the world and bring an end to all wars. Every link in the chain counted, I guessed, how small or big.

As my gaze followed Ellen to the door, my eyes stopped abruptly at a table by the entrance. Yet again, I had come across María and her mother. The little girl smiled at me and I winked.

Valur closed the front door of the apartment building behind him and shrugged when confronted with the fresh Icelandic summer breeze. Having lived abroad for a decade and a half, he was struggling to get used to the fact that the ideal dress for summer days was not simply a T-shirt—even at midsummer. Valur looked up between the midrise residential towers where he was staying this week. The sky was gray. Although it was not what he was used to these days, the weather could hardly be more typical for this part of the world at this time of the year. It was one of those days where it was uncertain if it would rain or not, but one thing was sure, it was going to be cloudy.

The weather was one of the parameters Valur had to keep in mind if he was to move back to Reykjavík. He had to make sure he would be able to accept it. There would not be as many sunny days in Reykjavík as he was used to enjoying either in Amsterdam or Barcelona. There would definitely be more cloudy days. More rain. More snow. More slush. Then there would be that indecisive constant drizzle that could go on for days without making up its mind if it was going to fall as proper rain or not. He should embrace the fact that there would be weeks where he would hardly see the sun. It was true that he sometimes complained about the suffocating summer heat by the Mediterranean, but he had to keep in mind that all in all Barcelona had a better climate than either Amsterdam or Reykjavík. It was also one of the few positive aspects of his frequent journeys between Barcelona and Amsterdam that he could choose to spend an extra couple of days in Holland if Catalonia was too warm.

Valur walked across the parking lot between the apartment buildings and made his way toward Borgartún. It was arguably among the denser parts of Reykjavík, and by urban theories it should be accompanied by an active street life. However, there were few people out and about on this Tuesday morning. The only sign of life was a constant stream of cars moving up and down the street. Come to think of it, this was typical of Reykjavík street life. The few people who ventured outside stayed inside their automobiles. What was it about his fellow countryfolk and cars? Did they really like them so much or were they merely caught in a situation where the urban design with low density and mighty suburbs made it too difficult to break out of those motorized steel cages? Maybe it was a chicken and egg problem where few people used sustainable transport because the infrastructure was lacking and no politician dared invest in infrastructure for sustainable transport since there were so few users—so few voters, so few votes. In any case, cars were not Valur's cup of tea and he wondered how much he would miss the street life of the two cities he was contemplating leaving behind. He would miss the bustling squares of Barcelona, the busy pavements, the small shops that he could reach on foot, the greengrocer, the butcher, the wineshop. He would miss the cycling in Amsterdam, the canal walks past ever-changing gables, and, last but not least, the Vondelpark picnics. He would miss the cities where life took place in public spaces—not only indoors, be it doors to houses or doors to cars. He imagined how different it would be if he were wandering about Barcelona today. He would sit down for a coffee in a café on a busy square, enjoying watching people as they went about their business in the midmorning sun. If he wasn't in a Tuesday morning meeting, that is.

As Valur reached the open area around Höfði he stopped for a moment to look over to the mountains across the *blue straits*. The scene that had inspired so many poets—one describing the mountain ranges as purple dreams on a spring night. The mountain view, the straits, the islands—one could hardly imagine a better frame for a city. Reykjavík was an urban area in close proximity to nature, and the wilderness was no doubt one of the main attractions of Iceland, not only for tourists but also for himself. He loved the endless views of emptiness. The quiet nature. For sure it was easy to get to the mountains from Barcelona. The Pyrenees were only a couple hours away by train. However, even if both Reykjavík and Barcelona had an easy route to mountains, it was not the same. There was not the same sense of isolation on the Iberian Peninsula as in the Icelandic highlands. As much as Valur didn't like the lack of people on the streets of Reykjavík, he did not like the abundance of people in the Pyrenees. He realized he was an extremist in that sense. For him there were only two possible states of being. The big city with its crowds and dense street life on one hand and untouched nature on the other, where he could be alone or with a small group of close friends, with a low probability of running into other people.

Valur was really looking forward to the trip he had coming up the following week. He was traveling with the usual group of friends to the remote northwestern part of Iceland where they were going to spend eight days walking in the wilds without ever seeing a town, without ever coming across a human-inhabited place. It was going to be a week on the border between civilization and the uninhabited ice sheet of the North Pole. Valur missed these outings. The group did at least two weeklong trips every year and then there were the more frequent, but shorter, weekend excursions. Valur tried to catch at least one of the longer trips every year, but he could not make it for the weekend escapes. It would be so much easier if he lived in Reykjavík.

When Valur reached Laugavegur, the street got livelier and there were more people around. They were mostly tourists, though, and he wondered if he himself felt more like a local or a tourist. The scene was in some ways familiar, but at the same time quite novel. He struggled to identify with the place. So much had changed in the past fifteen years. Icelandic society had evolved, and he had matured too. There was something about the way of life in Iceland that he could not relate to. He liked living a modest lifestyle in a small flat, without the luxuries of a microwave, television, dishwasher, or dryer. He didn't own a car or have a mortgage. Things in Iceland were different. Here he felt that everyone was expected to have the same lifestyle, with their house and garden, children and cars, dishwashers and dogs. Valur wanted to be agile—free to move around—free to live in the present without having to think about the future. He was afraid that if he moved to Reykjavík he would plant his feet too rigidly into the infertile Icelandic soil.

At the bottom of Bankastræti Valur headed toward the harbor where Harpa, the relatively new concert hall, stood. He paused on the hill in front of the hall and admired the fancy construction. The building itself was an impressive glass structure influenced by the hexagonal rocks found in abundance in Icelandic nature, but the surrounding was not as stunning—a mix of vacant lots and vast empty holes waiting to be filled with the foundations of new buildings. It was now four years since the 2008 economic crisis had put construction on hold, and there were not many signs of the pace picking up anytime soon. The square in front of the concert hall was as depressing as the building was stunning. Most of it was covered with black asphalt, not so different from an empty parking lot. In order to prevent drivers from mistaking it for parking, a number of concrete blocks had been scattered over the surface. Valur did like the iconic Icelandic landscape of black sand as far as the eye could reach. However, this was not the venue for the desert. Just as the black sands was uninviting to human populations, this ocean of asphalt was equally harsh. This was the city. This should be a welcoming place for people. There were admittedly a few benches scattered across the square but nothing to attract interesting city life. No vegetation. No street cafés. Nothing. Valur felt sad. He really wanted to be in love with Reykjavík. He longed to be excited. It would make his decision to relocate to the city so much easier.

Valur walked across Lækjartorg, down Hafnarstræti, heading for the Reykjavík Art Museum. He needed to clear his mind. He needed a mental diversion. He had to stop thinking about the relocation for a while, and a museum was an ideal distraction.

★ ★ ★ ★ ★

Although it was a cloudy summer morning with tourist season in full swing, he was alone in the big hall. There was a complete silence apart from the squeaking from under the rubber soles of his shoes as he walked across the glossed concrete floor. Valur felt a relaxing sensation go through his body and ease the tension that had been building up for the past few days.

Visiting the museum had been a good idea. The theme of the current exhibition was art from everyday life. The advertised goal was to find the border between things we consider artwork and things we use as part of our daily routine.

At the center of the hall, Valur stopped by quite an ordinary armchair, placed next to a big sign asking guests not to sit on the artwork. He stared at the armchair. Was this art or was this just an item from everyday life? That was an intriguing question. What was art, anyway? Can an ordinary armchair in the middle of a room be art? For sure there was design in the chair. But art? Where did the line lie between art and design? Between design and manufacturing? Was the design present in every produced iteration, or just in the original prototype? Plato would surely have had an answer for that.

"Is this art?"

Valur jumped. He had not heard anyone enter the hall, and the voice seemed to originate from right behind his back. He turned around and faced a woman standing a few feet away. She was below average height and slim. Her chestnut hair was cut short, at chin height, and her bright gray-blue eyes pulled at his attention like magnets. Her skin was pale and smooth. She was smiling. On one hand she had a childish look to her but something in her aspect made Valur guess she was about his age—recently past her midthirties.

"Quite frankly, I have no clue," Valur replied after he had recovered from the startle. "I was actually pondering that exact question. I find it hard to see a chair in the middle of a room as an object of art. If this chair is called art, then anything can be labeled as art. Can't it?"

"I'm not sure if it's that simple," the woman said as she moved closer and walked around the chair to view it better. "Maybe the art is not so much in the chair itself. The artist could be challenging us to look beyond the chair and ask ourselves a different set of questions. Isn't it too narrow to focus solely on the chair as an object of art? Could it be that the art lies in the combination of the chair and the sign? In the contrast put forward by not allowing people to use the chair for the purpose it was made? Maybe the purpose of the artist is to make us choose between two incompatible choices. Maybe the artist really wants us to sit down, even if we are told not to do so."

She finished her walk around the chair and sat down. Valur could feel the hair on his arms rise and a nervous tension spread through his body. "You can't do that," he whispered, looking about the room to see if there were any guards. "Someone might see you!"

"I doubt that," she said grinning. "I think the artist wants you to think about the contrast between the things you should do and the things you want to do. The contrast between the things you think you should do and the things you really want to do. The contrast between what you want to want and what you really want. People are asking themselves the wrong questions all the time. They are obsessed with asking the questions that lead them to the conclusions they want to reach."

"Are you the artist?" Valur asked, calming down a little, suspecting this scene was all a part of the show.

"You don't remember me, do you?" the woman asked, staring at him with those hypnotizing gray-blue eyes.

"No, should I?" Valur answered, wondering if she was an old classmate from high school or even elementary school. No, he could not locate her in his memory.

"It's me, Ugla," she said. "Don't you remember? Your old friend."

"Ugla?" Valur was taken aback. The scene had been confusing before but was now turning into something too surrealistic to believe. "Ugla? My invisible friend from childhood?"

"Do I look invisible to you?"

"No," Valur admitted, though unconvinced.

"Then I'd prefer if you referred to me—" she said, pausing for a moment—"simply as your friend."

Valur was silent, his eyes fixed on the woman sitting in the armchair in front of him. She stared back, grinning. Valur closed his eyes and took a deep breath. Ugla, his imaginary friend from childhood. He smiled. He had not thought of her in a long time. In fact, he had no personal recollections of her. He remembered her only through the stories his parents repeated so often. According to them, he and Ugla frequently played together. He had his parents put a plate for her at the dining table, as she joined them for dinner from time to time. She even traveled with the family. Until one summer when they were on holiday in Ireland, she disappeared. He stopped mentioning her. He stopped playing with her. It appeared as if she had disappeared entirely from his mind—ceased to be a figment of his imagination. No one knew what had terminated their friendship.

Valur opened his eyes again. Ugla was still there. Sitting in the armchair, laid back and relaxed, staring at him.

"Why don't we go somewhere nice and have a drink," she said, standing up from the chair. "We have plenty of catching up to do."

★ ★ ★ ★ ★

Valur and Ugla left the museum and walked back into the chilly Icelandic summer morning. Noon was still over an hour away and there would be no problem finding a quiet space to catch up. Valur suggested they go to the restaurant in the Falcon House as it was reasonably close by and, quite frankly, one of the few places he actually knew in town. He visited too infrequently to keep up with the fast turnover in the gastronomic scene.

"I'll go to the restroom," Ugla said as they had found themselves a nice table by a window, overlooking Ingólfstorg Square.

Valur sat down and studied the wine list. He was no expert but managed to recognize two reds on offer, a Spanish Crianza from Rioja and an Argentine Malbec from Mendoza.

"We'll have a bottle of the Malbec," Valur said to the waiter as he came over to the table. "And two glasses."

Valur could not help grinning. It was just as in his parents' stories where he felt he had to ask to have the table set for Ugla.

"Should I bring the wine now, or wait until your party arrives?" the waiter asked.

"Bring it now," Valur replied. "We arrived together. She just went to the bathroom and will be right back."

"Sure, of course," the waiter said, lifting his eyebrows. "As you wish."

The waiter returned with the bottle of wine and two glasses. He poured Valur a small glass for tasting. Valur let the wine roll around on his tongue for a while before accepting it. The waiter filled his glass and went about his business. Valur reached for the bottle and poured a half-full glass for Ugla.

"So, what brings you to Iceland?" Ugla asked as she returned from the bathroom. "I thought you were living in Barcelona, or was it Amsterdam?"

"Yes, I mostly live in Barcelona, but I also spend a lot of time in Amsterdam, for work. I'm just visiting."

"To Amsterdam and Barcelona," Ugla said, raising her glass for a toast. "Sounds like a nice combination."

"Cheers!" said Valur, lifting his glass. "It is. But what about you? Weren't we in Ireland last time we saw each other?"

"Yes we were, but I have no fixed place of residence. I wander around. Go where I'm needed. I usually do short stints in each place. Now I'm on a project in Reykjavík. I guess it will be a short stay, though. And you?"

"I'll be staying a couple of weeks."

"Business or pleasure?"

"Both. I'm going on a hiking trip with my friends next week, but I'm also here for a job. Yesterday I had an interview with a local company."

Thinking about the job interview, Valur felt butterflies in his stomach. Was he really this nervous about getting the job? Or was it the effect of drinking wine before lunch? In reality, he had no reason to be nervous. He had had much tougher interviews in the past. This one had been pretty easy in comparison. It was as if the job description had been written to perfectly match his education and work experience. The interview had gone really well and he felt a good vibe among the people. The chemistry had been right on so many levels. If anything, it had been too good to be true. It was a brand-new chemical engineering startup where he would be able to focus his energy exclusively on experimenting with natural chemicals under inspiration from Icelandic geothermal areas. The product was based on a concept he had been thinking about for a while. It would be a great contrast to the large multinational chemical giant where he currently spent more time in boring meetings and dealing with company politics than actually doing chemistry.

"Hopeful?" Ugla asked, interrupting his thoughts.

"About what?" Valur had forgotten she was there and what they had been talking about.

"The job, of course."

"Oh, yes. No. I mean yes. Both. Yes and no. I'm torn. On one side I'm hopeful that I'll get it. On the other... I don't know... I hope that I won't. It's complicated."

"Is the job not interesting enough?"

"No, it's not that. I mean yes, it's interesting. If anything, it's kind of a dream job for me."

"So, it's almost certain you'll get it?"

"Yes, I think so."

"That's great then!"

"I don't know."

"Why not?"

"I'd have to move to Reykjavík."

"What's wrong with Reykjavík?"

"I'm not sure. I'm not sure I like the city. I'm not sure I fit into the Icelandic mentality anymore."

"Why not?"

"I enjoy the modest urban lifestyle I maintain in Barcelona. I like to be able to have breakfast outside on a terrace all year round."

"How often do you have breakfast on a terrace in Barcelona?"

"Hardly ever, really."

"So?"

"That's not the issue. It's more about the concept. I would like to have the option. I just don't visualize myself in Reykjavík."

"Why not?"

"Many things. For one thing, I like a car-free lifestyle. My parents' town is an hour's drive from Reykjavík. My friends live all over the capital area, split between be city center, the suburbs, and the satellites. It would be madness getting around."

"Then why move?"

"For two years I've been casually thinking about returning to Iceland. I want to spend more time with my parents. I have a very close group of friends here. I miss them. I miss spending time with them, hiking, enjoying nature."

"I see," Ugla said, putting up a soothing smile that made Valur relax.

"I don't like the choice. For two years I've avoided addressing the question of whether I really want to live in Iceland, brushing it away by quite rightfully claiming that there were no jobs for me here. No jobs that fit my expertise, that is. I convinced myself that I had specialized myself away from the Icelandic job market. Therefore, I did not have to choose between the big city and my hometown. There wasn't a choice to make. Then, a few weeks ago, this company approached me and invited me for an interview."

"And since the interview went well, you can no longer hide," Ugla concluded, looking Valur in the eyes and reading his thoughts. "You cannot hide behind the excuse that there are no jobs for you in Iceland. You have to make up your mind. You have to make a decision."

"Exactly!" Deep inside Valur hoped the answer from the job interview would be negative. He hoped he wasn't the right person for the job and he wouldn't get it. Then he wouldn't have to answer any of those difficult questions. He could hit the snooze button once again. He could postpone the decision of whether to move back to Iceland or stay in Barcelona. He found the choice hard. Both options had their pluses and minuses. Neither option was clearly better than the other. "I want to spend more time with my friends and family, but I also want to live in a real city."

"What's real?" Ugla asked.

"Isn't it a bit ironic that you of all people would cast a doubt upon my notion of reality?"

"You're saying I'm not real?"

"I don't know," Valur sighed.

"What I'm saying is that sometimes it's not easy to distinguish between what's real and what's not. We find it hard to make a distinction between what we want to want and what we really want."

"I'm not sure it's that deep or philosophical," Valur said. "I think it's a quite straightforward conflict of constraints. In any case, I was trying not to think about it for a while. Can we change the subject?"

"Sure," Ugla said. "How's your brother?"

"My brother?" Valur felt his body tense, the blood rush to his face, and his voice get louder. "What has he got... got to do with anything?"

"Take it easy. I was just asking," Ugla said, shrugging. "I was just curious since I remembered you having an older brother. A year your senior, no?"

"Yes, I did have an older brother," Valur replied. "I do have an older brother. I guess he's fine."

"So you haven't been in touch with him since you arrived?"

"No," Valur replied, looking away and over the square. "I've been busy."

"And the fact that your brother married your childhood crush—the love of your life—has nothing to do with your doubt about relocating to Iceland?"

Valur closed his eyes and felt as if the world was spinning around in his head. This was not happening. He was not being lectured by an entity that didn't even exist—from some imaginary creature that seemed able to enter and exit his life at its own will every few decades. What did she know about what he thought or did not think? What he wanted to want or what he really wanted?

★ ★ ★ ★ ★

When Valur opened his eyes again and looked across the table, Ugla was gone. All he sat across was a half-full glass of red wine. His own glass was empty. He poured the last drops of wine into his glass and leaned back in the chair. He was tipsy, but his head was clearer than before. He had made a decision. She had been right, after all. He did not have to wait for any more answers. He was not going to take the job if they offered it to him. He was not ready to move back to Reykjavík. He was not ready to face reality.

I look out the window and into a gray winter day. There are dark clouds hanging low in the sky, but at the moment it is neither raining nor snowing. In the street outside, cars drive past in a continuous stream, throwing dirty slush onto the sidewalk.

I'm in the big city. I'm in Reykjavík. That I know for certain. I also know I've been here for a while. I've been here for weeks, months, years. I don't know exactly.

I look away from the window and explore my surroundings. Right in front of me, on the other side of the room, there is a chest of drawers, next to a bed, neatly made up with white linen. The surrounding walls are also white. The inside of my world is white and clean but the outside is gray and gloomy. What has become of the colors of my life? The green grass, the blue sky, the yellow flowers...

I look at my hands, the old wrinkled skin. My life's hard labor has taken its toll. I'm not the strong farmer I used to be. I clench my fists and unclench them again. I still have some strength left in my body, so I put my hands on the arms of the chair, push myself up, and walk slowly across the room.

I gently stroke the top of the chest. Just like my own hands, the old wood is worn. I close my eyes and enter the work shed where my father is sanding wood. I watch him for hours, shaping the raw material into this beautiful chest of drawers. For the ten-year-old boy I am, it seems like magic.

I open my eyes and gaze at the collection of photos scattered across the top of the chest. I pick up one of the frames and hold it in my trembling hands. There we are, together in front of our farmhouse by the fjord, young and smiling. I'm wearing a gray suit and a white shirt. You're wearing a blue dress and a white apron. I know the dress is blue, even if the photo is black and white. I bought it in the cooperative the autumn after we got married. It was the first gift I gave you as my wife.

The photo is taken on our first wedding anniversary. The photographer is Danish. He is traveling around the island, documenting Icelandic country life, and makes a stop at our farm, maybe by chance, maybe deliberately.

"Why don't we invite you to a small celebration?" you ask the photographer's interpreter. "I'll bake some pancakes and brew some fresh coffee. It's our first wedding anniversary. We got married one year ago. On this day."

While we eat, you talk endlessly about the life by the fjord, the landscape, the people, the weather, the customs.

"You'll have to pay old Snjólfur a visit," you say. "He's a curious old loner... If you pass that ridge and go down into the valley below you might see some wild reindeer... You're lucky that the wind is blowing from the northwest today. It may be a bit chilly but look at the clear blue sky! Imagine if it were blowing from the southeast. It would be warmer but raining... The large stone down there by the road is the biggest elfish castle by the fjord. The road workers didn't dare touch it. That's why the road takes such a large bend around it..."

The poor interpreter can hardly find time to bite into his pancake, but the photographer must like your initiative because he sends us the photo all the way from Copenhagen as a token of his gratitude.

I put the frame back onto the chest of drawers and turn around to head back across the room. There's a young man sitting in the chair next to mine. He looks at me and smiles. He's wearing a dark-gray suit and a white shirt. For a moment I think he looks just like me in the Danish photographer's photo. He's like the ghost of myself visiting from the past.

I walk over to him, slowly, one step at a time. When I reach my destination, I turn around, carefully put my hands on the arms of the chair, and ease myself into the seat.

"And who are you, young man?" I ask, turning to the young man.

"Grandpa, it's me, Emil," he answers. "Sóley's son."

I close my eyes and see Sóley running around the grassy slopes of the hills above the farmhouse. She's five years old. It's spring. I'm fixing a barbed-wire fence that got damaged by the heavy snow during the winter—the winter of 1944 to 1945. The snow retreated late. The hay reserves ran low. Rusty died that winter, the light-brown sheep with the rust-red dot on her forehead. Over the years, she had been a reliable source of healthy and strong lambs.

Sóley runs to me, smiling. I see excitement in her eyes. She's innocent and oblivious of the effects of the harsh winter.

"Look, Dad, I found a *sóley*," she says, laughing, revealing a meadow buttercup in her hand. "My flower. But now it's yours. I'm giving it to you."

"Thank you!" I take the flower and bring it to my chest where it sticks to my woolen sweater. "You know I already own the most beautiful *sóley* in the world."

"I know," Sóley replies, shrugging, and she returns to skipping between the rocks and grassy knolls. She runs around, knocking on stones, greeting the hidden people who live inside.

I open my eyes and look at the young man sitting next to me. So he's the son of my little Sóley. I can believe that. He has the same eyes and the same smile.

"Now she's gone, your grandmother," I say to my grandson. "One of these days I'll be traveling east to attend her funeral."

"Grandma's funeral was a month ago," says the young man.

I close my eyes and see the small church at the doorstep of our farmhouse. I'm cutting the grass of the front lawn. The Icelandic flag is flying at the middle of the pole. I'm getting the church ready for a funeral. My eyes wander up to the farmhouse. You're inside baking pancakes and brewing coffee, preparing the reception. From the back of the church I can hear the digging of a grave.

I remember the day clearly. Your father goes to check the nets out on the fjord. It's a calm autumn morning. I'm going to go with him but am called to lend old Snjólfur a hand with harvesting the last of his hay. "Go and help old Snjólfur," your father says. "I'll take care of the nets." Midday the weather suddenly turns, the wind starts blowing, and rain starts pouring. Nobody knows exactly what happens out on the fjord, but your father doesn't make it back.

I open my eyes and look out the window. I'm in Reykjavík. It's snowing. The traffic moves slowly down the street outside. There's a long line of cars inching forward at a snail's pace. The drivers seem restless and I can feel the tension rising as they look impatiently ahead, longing to reach their destination faster than the weather permits.

I look away from the window and explore the white-painted surroundings. There's a young man sitting in the chair next to me. His blond hair, blue eyes, and friendly smile remind me of myself when I was his age.

"And who are you, young man?" I ask to satisfy my curiosity.

"I'm Emil. Your grandson. Son of Sóley."

I close my eyes. I'm standing on the recently mowed lawn in front of the church. It's summer. The sun is shining and the flag is flying in the summer breeze at the top of the pole. Sóley and I walk hand in hand toward the church. I'm wearing my Sunday suit and she's wearing a white dress. We look at each other and smile. I cannot believe how fast she has gone from being a small girl skipping between stones in the hills above the farm to a young woman, on her way to walk down the aisle—into a new chapter in her life— into holy matrimony. I open my eyes and look at my grandson.

"It's nice of you to visit," I tell him. "Have you traveled far?"

"No, I live in West Town. It's only a few minutes' drive."

"And your mother? What news can you tell me of her?"

"She just went out into the hall to talk to the nurse. She'll be back shortly."

That's good to hear. I always like having my little Sóley around. Especially now when you have departed. It's good to see familiar faces.

"Your grandmother has left," I observe. "Soon I'll be traveling east to attend the funeral."

Emil smiles and nods his head. Maybe that's the reason he's here. He's going to drive me east. I look forward to being back in the countryside. I look forward to being back by your side at our farm by the fjord.

I close my eyes and am standing in the middle of the field with a wooden scythe in my hand. I'm cutting the grass under the warm August sun. You're walking slowly across the field, carrying a bag and a bottle.

"What a wonderful afternoon, my darling!" you exclaim as you approach. "I brought you lunch. Bread, pancakes, and coffee."

I put the scythe aside and greet you with a kiss. We sit down on the stones in the center of the field and I attend to my bread and coffee. I'm really hungry after the morning's hard labor. You talk of the fabrics you're going to buy at the cooperative this autumn— the curtains you want to replace. Before long, I finish my lunch and kiss you goodbye before you return to the house. I've got little time to lose. I must make the most of the dry and sunny weather, so I pick up the scythe and go back to cutting the grass.

I open my eyes. Sóley is sitting in the chair next to me. She's not the young girl she used to be but a mature woman. A young man is standing by her side. He reminds me of myself when I was his age. He reminds me of Sóley when she was his age. It must be her son, Emil.

"It's time for me to leave," I say. "It's time for me to go back to the countryside."

They both smile at me and Sóley caresses my old and veiny hand. I smile back and close my eyes. I feel the calm come over me. I'm going back—back where I belong.

Eindride walked by his wife's side through the wide door, into the ballroom where the company's annual Christmas party was already in full swing— her company's party. Passing through the doorframe, Ellinor's back straightened, her chin pushed up, and her pace slowed as she changed into her charm-the-clients gear. Eindride followed her through the crowd, through the endless stream of Hello, how are you?... Lovely to see you... This is my husband, Eindride... How are the kids?... You remember my husband, Eindride? The clients had barely enough time to look at him and nod in recognition before Ellinor would steer the talk away from family friendly small talk and on to business, I hear it was a good quarter, I believe the appetite for mergers will rise in the spring... Eindride didn't mind how little attention he got. He knew his role. This was not his night. He wasn't the type of person who has their own nights. His role was usually that of a supporting actor, a part of the surroundings, a part of the crowd. Tonight was Ellinor's night and it was written in the unwritten contract between husband and wife that they support each other. And so they did. Each in their own capacity.

Eindride followed his wife for a while before getting bored of being a pet on a leash, picked up a glass of red wine from a roaming waiter's tray, and drifted into the periphery of the room where he could observe the crowd—see if he spotted anyone he knew, anyone he recognized, anyone he could casually walk up to and start a conversation with. Not that he needed someone to talk to. He would be happy to stay on the edge of the scene and observe people, study their faces, their body language, their interaction with others. He would be content watching the social dynamic of the room as if he were enjoying a movie. However, he felt uncomfortable in that situation. Not because he was inherently uneasy with being an observer but because he knew people felt awkward by being observed by a member of their own species. They didn't mind the security cameras, the website cookies, and the mobile phone location tracking—or so he had read in an article on the Internet. People felt uncomfortable when a flesh-and-blood person observed them. That was considered inappropriate, weird, creepy. Eindride didn't want to be considered a weirdo—not at Ellinor's party.

The crowd looked the same as every year. Eindride recognized a few faces but could not spot anyone he was sufficiently familiar with to engage in a conversation. There was a large presence of wealthy-looking businesspeople, either current or prospective clients of Ellinor's law firm. It was not a gathering of the superrich, no one arrived by helicopter—at least not as far as Eindride knew. There was also a decent presence of what Eindride considered to be common people, friends of the law firm's partners, partners of the law firm's partners. Eindride had once even met the partner of a friend of a partner's partner. In particular there were many Norwegians.

Hello, I'm James, said a young man who had sneaked up beside Eindride while he was observing the crowd. Eindride, replied Eindride. Norwegian? Yes. Been in London long? How long had it been since they moved from Oslo? More than three years. This was Eindride's third Christmas party in London. It had been four years since Ellinor had said Eindride, darling, come here and sit down, I have some news. It had been four years since Eindride had thought Ellinor was about to tell him she was pregnant. It was she who didn't want to have children. She said children didn't match her career objectives. Eindride was more open to the idea although he didn't have a strong opinion on the subject. He was not a man of strong opinions in general. At least not about everyday things. Not that having children was an everyday thing, in a sense. But anyway, Ellinor had not told him she was pregnant when they sat down together in their all-white living room in Oslo—or had it been lime-white? She had told him she had received an incredibly exciting offer to set up the law firm's new office in London. A bit over three years, replied Eindride to the young man, came here with my wife, she's a partner in the firm. Ellinor? Yes. I didn't know she was Norwegian, said James, nodding his head as if to reinforce this new piece of knowledge, I just started last week, I'm with the firm, an intern. James and Eindride chatted for a while. There turned out to be quite a few things the young man was curious to know about Norway and Eindride tried his best to answer faithfully, just north of five million, oil, no, but the European Economic Area, the cheese cutter, football, skiing, and skating, Ole Gunnar Solskjær, but I guess that was before your time, Edvard Grieg and Edvard Munch, A-ha, also before your time, no, I don't believe Santa Claus lives there, or anywhere, for that matter. It was nice to meet you, said James finally when he had learned enough about Norway, I must continue my tour of mingling with the guests. It was nice to meet you too, Eindride replied and they shook hands on parting.

All the talking had made Eindride thirsty and he walked over to the bar and asked for another glass of red wine. So, you staff or client? asked a short elderly man as Eindride turned back to face the crowd after having his glass refilled. The man was wearing a black striped suit, white shirt, and a burgundy bow tie. Eindride guessed he was one of Ellinor's clients. One whom she advised on mergers and acquisitions, IPOs or whatever it was called, all that the firm offered. At home, they didn't talk that much about work. Instead, they talked about music and films— their common interests—the interests that had been the foundation of their relationship and still served as the glue. Eindride didn't recognize the man. Maybe a new client. Neither, answered Eindride, I'm the spouse of one of the partners, Ellinor. How lovely, the man continued as if he knew a thing or two about love, marriage, or the combination of the two. And what

is your line of business? the man asked. I'm a painter.
How lovely, what is your particular style? I am mostly
into collecting sculptures myself. Have I seen your
work somewhere? Did I tell you I am into collecting
sculptures? Yes I did, didn't I? Sculptures are not what
they used to be. Now there are more installations—
video installations, sound installations, and so on. I
collect them too. Just bought one piece last week. A
video installation of a woman smiling. It may sound
trivial and snobbish but a genuine smile is just so lovely,
it is truly art to catch it on film. You are a painter,
you said? What sort of works do you do? I myself
like impressionism. But hardly anyone does that sort
of work anymore. Last week I even heard some artist
are working in a post-contemporary style. Can you
believe that word? How can people have moved past
the contemporary? Are they painting in the future?
Are they selling an option to have a painting painted?
Just like they do on Wall Street?

On that philosophical question the man finished
his monologue at last and Eindride could answer the
original question. I mostly do monochrome acrylic
paint on concrete, he answered. How lovely, how
original, the man replied, I am not sure if I have
seen much of it. How do you classify that? Neo-
minimalism? We must be in touch to follow up. I
will get your details from Ellinor. Now I must dash.

Without another word the man bolted over to the other side of the room to pick up a new conversation—or to give another monologue. Ellinor always told Eindride to use the title *decorator* rather than *painter* when talking to her clients here in the UK. We must adapt to the local customs, she said. Eindride was not as good at adapting as Ellinor. He hadn't gone to university in Oxford. He didn't like the title *decorator*—even if it was the local custom. He didn't think of his work as decorating. He didn't decorate walls. He didn't arrange flowers and vases. He simply covered walls in paint. He was a painter, not a decorator.

Hey there, nice to see you again, said a man in Norwegian. Eindride remembered having seen him at last year's party. You look lost in thought, come over and have a chat, the man continued, inviting Eindride to a group of three people who looked somewhat familiar and were probably present last year as well. It's becoming a custom to meet like this every year, the man claimed. Eindride consented politely, while trying to remember who the man was and what his relation was to the firm. Was he the accountant, brother of the office manager? Oh boy, the traffic today, the man said to the group, it took me ages to drop the kids off at school this morning. So it was not the accountant. He didn't have any children at school, Eindride remembered from their chat the year before.

He had a grown-up son who studied civil engineering at university. When they met last year, the son had been about to go on a trip to the Gulf states to see some of the large-scale construction work going on in that part of the world. He was apparently fascinated by big engineering projects. He had always been captivated by construction. From the time he was a boy. Throughout his childhood, the accountant had often taken his son on excursions to building sites. Nowadays the tables had turned. The son took his father to see the sites where the most novel construction was taking place. They had a close relationship, father and son, even if they didn't live together anymore. The son lived with the accountant's ex-wife. The accountant lived with his husband. Or at least that had been the case last year when they spoke. It had been a pleasure talking to him. Eindride thought about how nice it would be to meet the accountant again this year. He was a much more interesting person to talk to than the group of three Eindride was facing at the moment, unable to be captured by their conversation.

Eindride took a big sip of his wine in order to have an excuse to leave the group. He felt awkward talking to people who were familiar but still strangers. There were too many unknowns in the discussion and he didn't feel comfortable asking questions to fill the gaps. It would only reveal the inconvenient truth that he didn't really remember who they were. It could become awkward if they knew who he was. It might reflect badly on Ellinor. Familiar strangers were the worst. It was much better to talk either to people he knew or to total strangers. Eindride lifted his empty glass to the group of three. Time for a refill, he said and headed for the bar.

While waiting in a queue to be served, Eindride looked about the room and saw Ellinor in a lively discussion with clients. For a moment their glances met. He smiled and nodded. She smiled and nodded. It was just a split-second interaction before she returned to her conversation. She looked content. The party was apparently unfolding according to plan. Eindride was happy for her.

Rather than getting his refill, Eindride put his empty glass on the counter, walked out into the main hallway, picked up his coat, and went into the cold December night. There was a jazz club around the corner and Eindride knew he would have a better time there—away from the company of familiar strangers.

Börkur Sigurbjörnsson is a computer scientist by training but complements his software development with writing fiction. Born and raised in Reykjavík, Börkur has over the past two decades lived in various places around Europe with prolonged says in Amsterdam, Barcelona, Burscheid, Düsseldorf, and London. His professional and private life has in addition brought him across the world, from Beijing to Bangalore, Berlin, Bariloche, Boston, Brno, and Buenos Aires—places where he has come across many strangers.

Börkur's previous works include *999 Abroad*, a collection of short stories published in 2012, and *Flash 52*, a collection of flash fiction published in 2017. He regularly publishes flash fiction and occasional short stories on his website, *Urban Volcano*, and tweets as @borkurdotnet.

https://urbanvolcano.net/
https://urbanvolcano.net/en/999-abroad/
https://urbanvolcano.net/en/flash-52/
https://urbanvolcano.net/en/talk-to-strangers/

www.ingramcontent.com/pod-product-compliance
Lightning Source LLC
Chambersburg PA
CBHW031152160726
47992CB00006B/2418